EARLY BIRD
STORIES

Izzy!
Wizzy!

Early ★ Reader

First American edition published in 2019 by Lerner Publishing Group, Inc.

An original concept by Elizabeth Dale
Copyright © 2019 Elizabeth Dale

Illustrated by Louise Forshaw

First published by Maverick Arts Publishing Limited

Maverick
arts publishing

Licensed Edition
Izzy Wizzy

Lerner Publications Company
A division of Lerner Publishing Group, Inc.
241 First Avenue North
Minneapolis, MN 55401 USA

For reading levels and more information, look up this title at www.lernerbooks.com.

Main body text set in Mikado a. Typeface provided by HVD Fonts.

Library of Congress Cataloging-in-Publication Data

Names: Dale, Elizabeth, 1952– author. | Forshaw, Louise, illustrator.
Title: Izzy! Wizzy! / by Elizabeth Dale ; illustrated by Louise Forshaw.
Description: First American edition. | Minneapolis : Lerner Publications, 2019. | Series: Early bird readers. Yellow (Early bird stories).
Identifiers: LCCN 2018017847 (print) | LCCN 2018033691 (ebook) | ISBN 9781541543348 (eb pdf) | ISBN 9781541541689 (lb : alk. paper) | ISBN 9781541546318 (pb : alk. paper)
Subjects: LCSH: Readers—Magic. | Readers (Primary) | Magic—Juvenile literature.
Classification: LCC PE1119 (ebook) | LCC PE1119 .D234 2019 (print) | DDC 428.6/2—dc23

LC record available at https://lccn.loc.gov/2018017847

Manufactured in the United States of America
1-45342-38992-6/27/2018

EARLY BIRD STORIES

Izzy! Wizzy!

Elizabeth Dale

Illustrated by
Louise Forshaw

Lerner Publications ◆ Minneapolis

I am called Izzy, and I am magic.

Look at all my magic spells . . .

Izzy! Wizzy!

I wish for a cat that I can hug!

Oh no! I cannot hug a slug!

Izzy! Wizzy! I wish for a pet hippo!

Eek! I do not need a pet toad!

Izzy! Wizzy! I wish for a doll to dress up!

No! No! I cannot dress up a snail!

Izzy! Wizzy! I wish for a dog.

No! A fish cannot run with me!

Izzy! Wizzy! I wish for a rabbit.

No! This crab will pinch me!

I am no good at magic spells!

Please let this wish work!

Izzy! Wizzy! I wish for a boat, please!

Look! That wish did happen—
and the rest did, too!

Quiz

1. When Izzy wishes for a cat, what does she get?
   a) A dog
   b) A mouse
   c) A slug

2. Why does Izzy want a doll?
   a) She wants to hug it.
   b) She wants to dress it up.
   c) She wants to swim with it.

3. What can't the fish do?
   a) Run
   b) Swim
   c) Blow bubbles

4. Where was the rabbit meant to come out from?
   a) A bed
   b) A boat
   c) A hat

5. Why does Izzy's last wish work?
   a) Because she said the magic word: "Please!"
   b) Because she said, "Abra Kadabra!"
   c) Because she was hungry

EARLY BIRD
STORIES™

Leveled for Guided Reading

Early Bird Stories have been edited
and leveled by leading educational
consultants to correspond with guided
reading levels. The levels are assigned
by taking into account the content,
language style, layout, and phonics
used in each book.

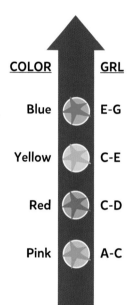

COLOR	GRL
Blue	E-G
Yellow	C-E
Red	C-D
Pink	A-C

DATE DUE

			PRINTED IN U.S.A.